This Little Tiger book
belongs to:

_____

_____

_____

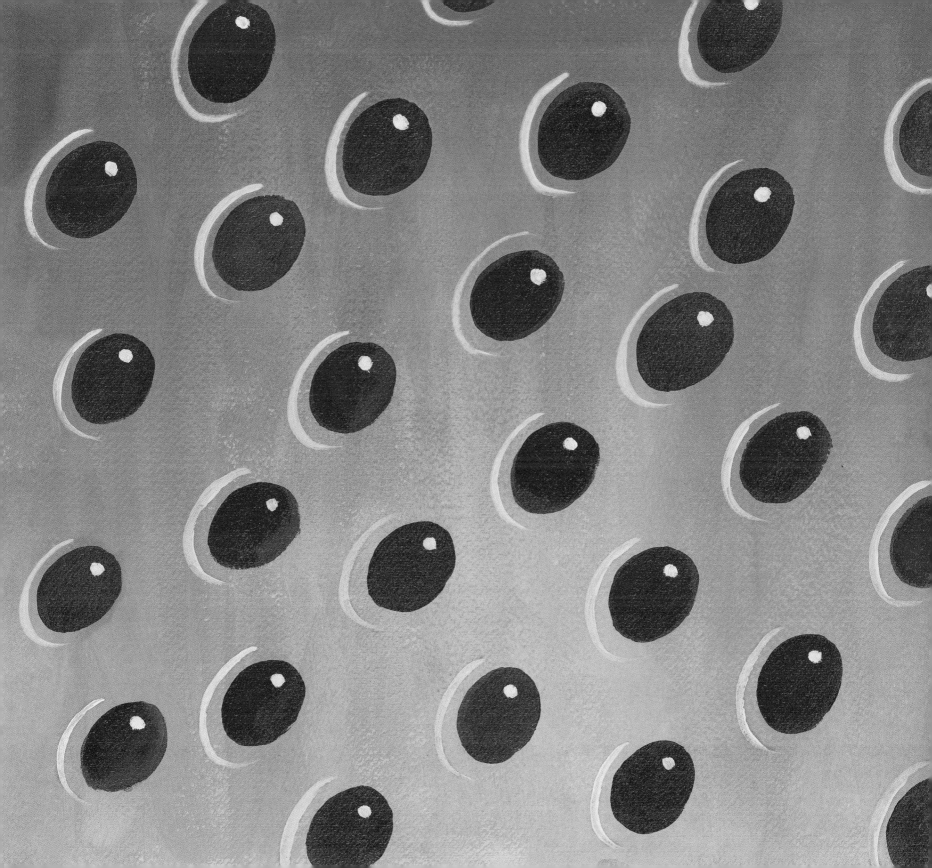

For my 'little' brother, Rob ~ S S

To 'Smelly Peter – The Great Pea Eater', who would probably have loved to have Percy as a pet! ~ J D

LITTLE TIGER PRESS
An imprint of Magi Publications
1 The Coda Centre
189 Munster Road
London SW6 6AW
www.littletigerpress.com

First published in Great Britain 2011
This edition published 2011
Text copyright © Steve Smallman 2011
Illustrations copyright © Joëlle Dreidemy 2011
Steve Smallman and Joëlle Dreidemy have
asserted their rights to be identified as the
author and illustrator of this work under
the Copyright, Designs and Patents Act, 1988
A CIP catalogue record for this book
is available from the British Library

ISBN 978-1-84895-135-8
Printed in Singapore
LTP/1500/0134/0910
2 4 6 8 10 9 7 5 3 1

Little Stinker!

Steve Smallman   Joëlle Dreidemy

LITTLE TIGER PRESS
London

Percy was a little fish,

    he wasn't smart or sporty.

He wasn't sweet and kind,

    in fact he could be rather naughty!

He wasn't that good-looking,

    he was small and kind of spotty.

But he was VERY good

    at blowing bubbles . . .

Percy's special bubbles often got him into trouble.

It's easy to make mischief with a well-timed botty bubble!

He liked to lie in wait as other fish were swimming past . . .

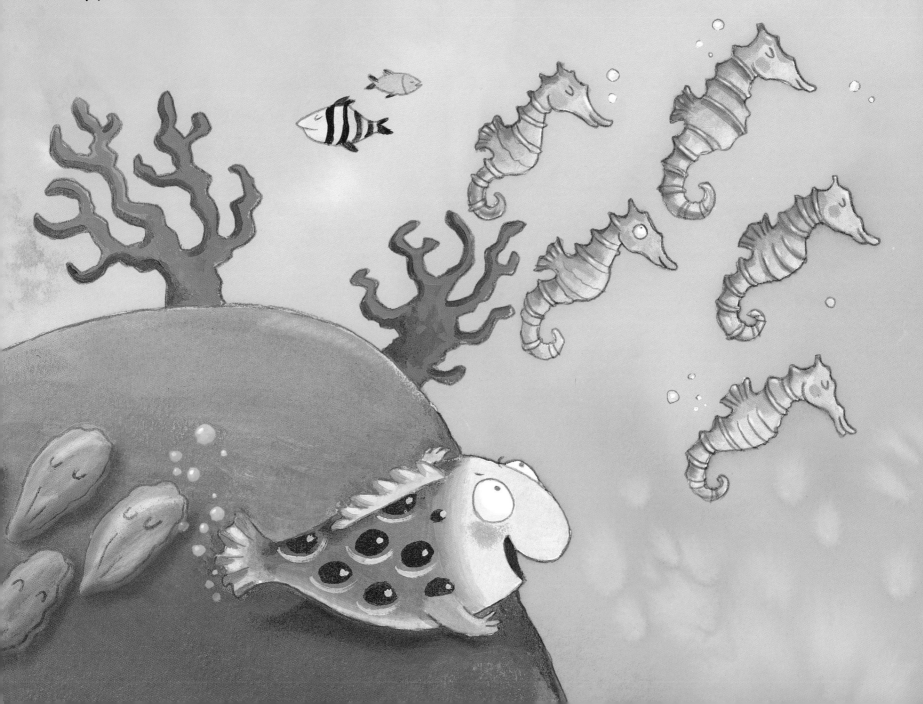

Then flip them upside down with an enormous

botty blast!

At school he always tried to cheat whenever they had races

By blowing stinky bubbles in the other fishes' faces.

Then using supersonic botty burping bubble power,

He'd shoot off like a ROCKET at a hundred miles an hour!

Sometimes during lessons he would wait for Mrs Trout
To turn her back and then he'd let a whiffy whopper out!

Then sneakily he'd use his tail to waft the beastly bubble
Behind poor Penny Pufferfish to get her into trouble.

One day a poor old hermit crab was reeling from the smell

Of the bubbly little 'present' Percy'd left inside his shell.

"That rotten **little stinker!**" cried the crab.

"Oh, what a pong!

"Hey, Percy!" cried the hermit crab.

"If you think you're so clever,

Why don't you try to blow the biggest

botty bubble EVER?"

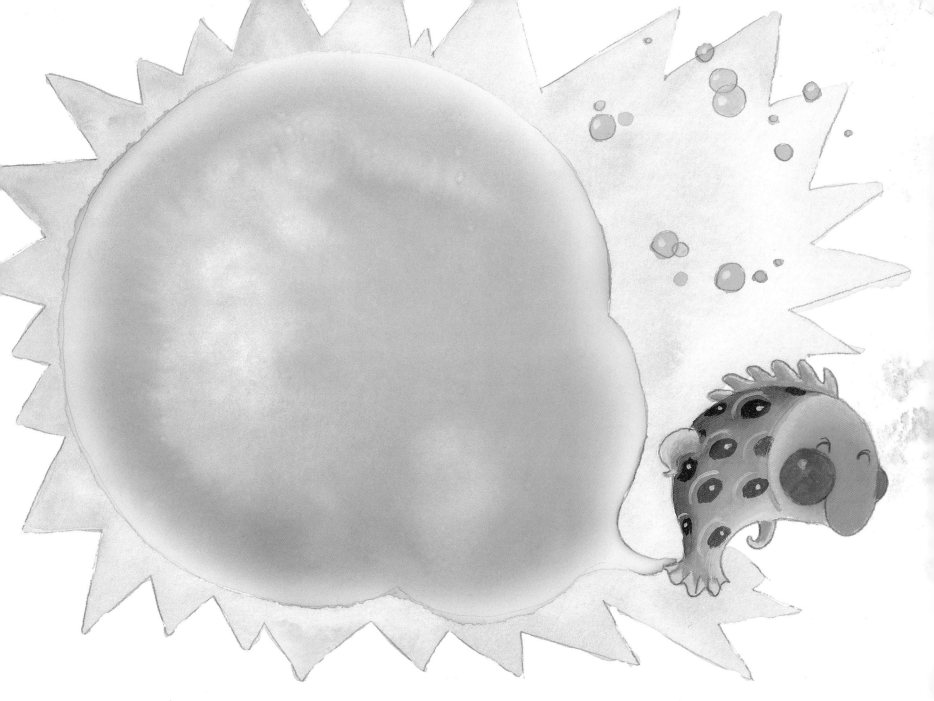

Percy's face went purple from the pressure as he tried it.

Then, **BLAAARp!**

he blew a **HUGE** one...

. . . and the crab pushed him inside it!

"It worked!" he shouted.

"Look that trumpy troublemaker's trapped!"

And all the other underwater creatures

cheered and clapped!

"Get me out!" gasped Percy, going greener by the minute

As the bubble bibble bobbled **UP and UP**

with **Percy** in it.

Then, suddenly the hermit crab dived back into his shell.
"LOOK OUT!" the others cried and
tried to hide themselves as well.

"Oh see those razor teeth," they gasped,
"those evil eyes ... good grief!
It's Two Ton Tom the tiger shark,

The tiger shark saw Percy and said, "Mmmmm, a juicy snack!"
And opened up his massive mouth and moved in to attack!
"Dinner time!" he laughed
but just before his jaws could close...

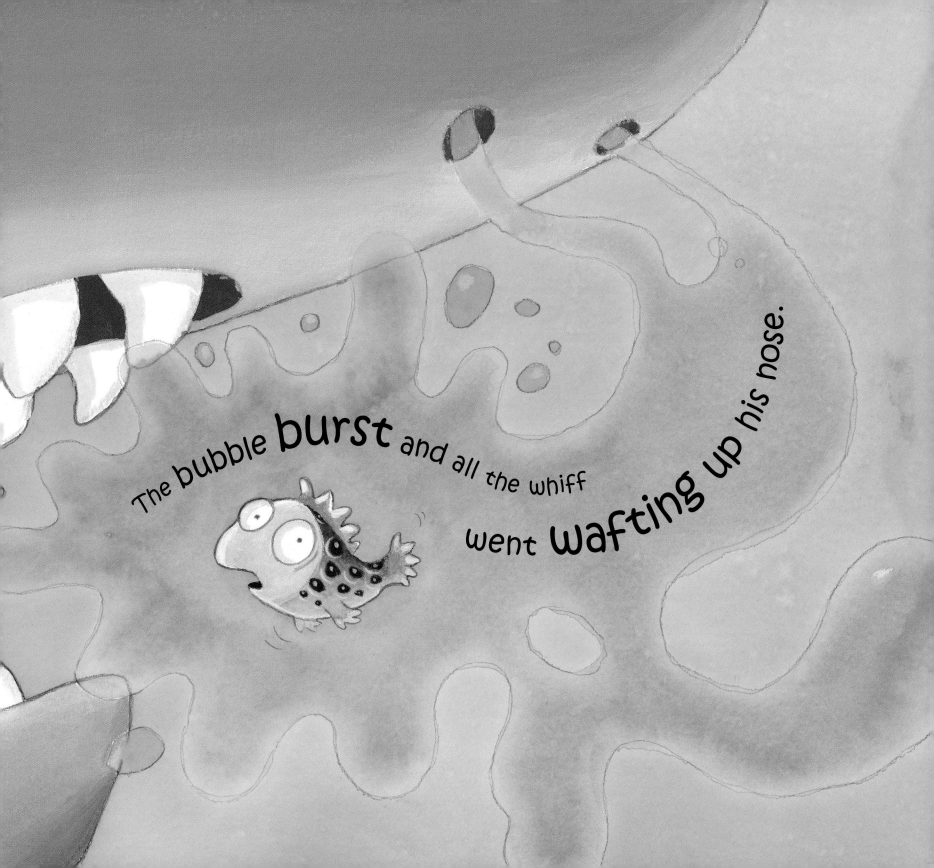

The shark swam off,
"Hooray for Percy!" all the fishes cried.
And Percy felt a warm and tingly
feeling deep inside.

"You must be feeling proud!"

suggested Hermit Crab and grinned.

"Well maybe," Percy said. "But, then again it could be . . .

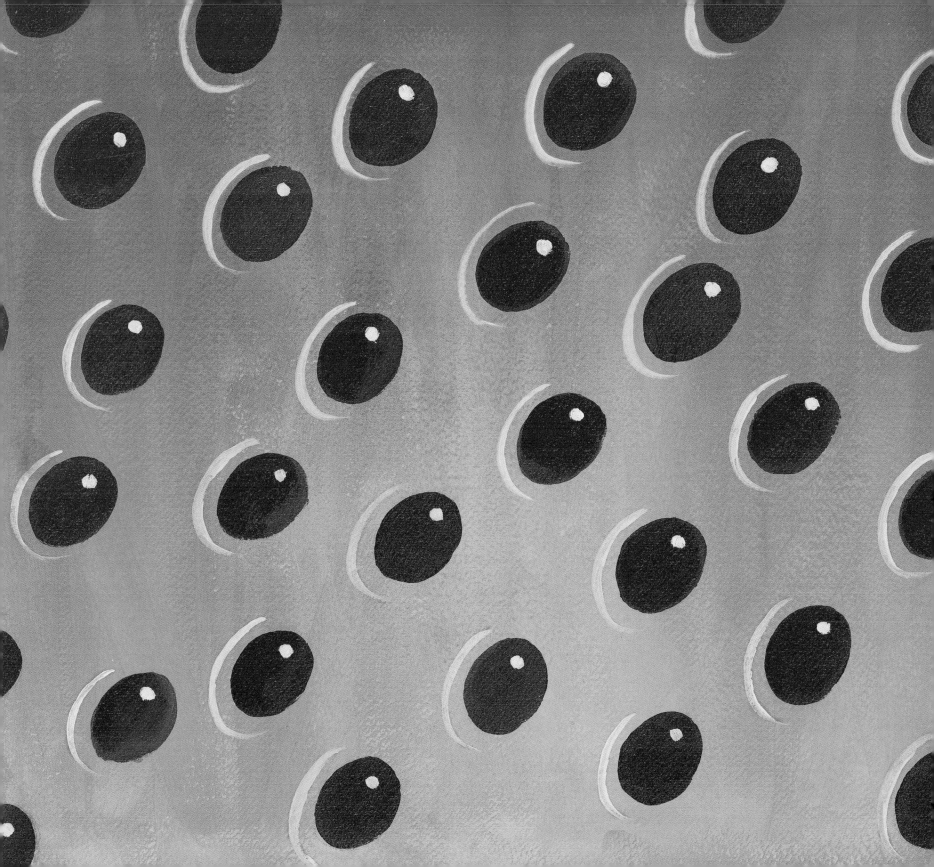